FRANK'S
MAGIC
FOOTBALL

BY FRANK LAMPARD

FRANKIE'S MAGIC FOOTBALL

THE GREAT SANTA RACE
FRANK LAMPARD

LITTLE, BROWN BOOKS FOR YOUNG READERS
www.lbkids.co.uk

LITTLE, BROWN BOOKS FOR YOUNG READERS

First published in Great Britain in 2015 by Hodder & Stoughton

1 3 5 7 9 10 8 6 4 2

A CIP catalogue record for this book
is available from the British Library.

ISBN 978-0-34913-209-9

Typeset in Cantarell by M Rules
Printed and bound in Great Britain by
Clays Ltd, St Ives plc

The paper and board used in this book are made
from wood from responsible sources.

MIX
Paper from
responsible sources
FSC
www.fsc.org
FSC® C104740

Little, Brown Books for Young Readers
An imprint of
Hachette Children's Group
Part of Hodder & Stoughton
Carmelite House
50 Victoria Embankment
London EC4Y 0DZ

An Hachette UK Company
www.hachette.co.uk

www.hachettechildrens.co.uk

*To my mum Pat, who encouraged me
to do my homework in between kicking
a ball all around the house, and is still
with me every step of the way.*

Welcome to a fantastic
Fantasy League – the greatest
football competition ever held
in this world or any other!

You'll need four on a team,
so choose carefully. This is a lot
more serious than a game in the
park. You'll never know who your
next opponents will be, or
where you'll face them.

So lace up your boots, players,
and good luck! The whistle's
about to blow!

The Ref

PART ONE

CHAPTER 1

Frankie pulled his jumper over his head and set it on the bench. Even though it was December 23rd, he was sweating. He had been playing football in the park all afternoon with his friends Charlie and Louise. Now, the sun was starting to go down.

"No chance of a white Christmas this year," said Louise,

balancing the football on her head.

The goal had been set up between two tree trunks. Charlie stood in position and clapped his goalie gloves together. "Come on, have a shot," he called. "You haven't got one past me yet."

Frankie saw a glint in Louise's eye. She let the ball fall and caught it on her ankle.

"Is that a challenge?" she said.

Charlie dropped into a crouch and spread his arms, grinning. Frankie's friend wasn't lying. He'd been amazing all day, diving and jumping and blocking the ball.

Louise took position like she was about to shoot, then at the last minute she slid the ball to Frankie. As Charlie turned to face him, Frankie stabbed his toe underneath the ball and sent it in a soft looping chip over the goalkeeper's head.

Charlie flapped but couldn't reach it, and the ball sailed over his outstretched arms. It landed beyond the goal line. Charlie's face flushed red.

"Don't worry," said Frankie, going to clap his friend on the shoulder. "It was a lucky shot."

The sound of shuffling footsteps made them all turn. A paunchy man in a tracksuit was jogging slowly along the path towards them, bent over and panting. Frankie recognised the scruffy trainers, and the dog trotting on a lead.

"Hi, Dad!" he called. "Hi, Max!"

Frankie's dad waved weakly.

Max, Frankie's dog, broke free and ran towards them, the lead trailing behind him. He jumped up and placed his paws on Frankie's legs. As Frankie stroked Max behind his ears, his dad started stretching and touching his toes.

"How come your dad's running?" whispered Charlie. "I've never seen him exercise before."

Frankie chuckled. "He's training for the town Santa Race tomorrow," he said. "It's a circuit around the park, dressed like Santa Claus."

Charlie frowned. "Will he make it?" he asked.

"I hope so," said Frankie. "He's been training really hard since November."

At last, his dad strolled over.

"Good luck tomorrow in the Santa Race," said Louise.

"Thanks, Lou," said Frankie's dad. "I'll need it!" He paused to catch his breath. "I came to tell you, Mr Harris next door is switching on his lights soon. Do you want to come and watch?"

"Sure!" said Frankie. Every year their next-door neighbour had the best light display in town. Frankie's dad always said their electricity bill must be through the roof.

Frankie picked up Max's lead.

"Don't forget your ball," said his dad.

Frankie couldn't believe he almost had. His dad didn't know that the football had magical powers – if someone else found it, anything could happen! He tucked the ball under his arm, and they set off home.

By the time they reached Frankie's road, the sky was dark. There was already a crowd gathered in front of the Harris house. The lights were all strung up, with cables stretching across the lawn and the front of the house. Bulbs hung from the upstairs windows, and the front door was covered in holly wreaths. Spaced across the lawn stood four model penguins. Mr Harris was up a ladder in front of his garage, fixing a life-size Santa and sled, complete with two reindeer. Next door, Frankie's house just had a few lights twinkling along the windowsills.

"It doesn't seem quite right — penguins with no snow," said Charlie.

"It's wrong," muttered Louise. "Santa's from the North Pole, but penguins are from the South Pole.

You'd never find them next to each other like that."

"Don't tell Mr Harris," replied Frankie's dad. "He takes his lights very seriously."

Frankie grinned. As he reached the house, Mr Harris spotted him. "Keep that football away from my lights," he grumbled.

Frankie nodded. "Yes, Mr Harris." His neighbour got angry because Frankie's football was always flying over the back fence and squashing his flowers.

"Done!" said Mr Harris, climbing down. "Right everyone — two minutes till I flick the switch!"

Frankie's mum and Kevin joined the crowd. Frankie's mum was carrying a tray of mince pies for everyone. Mrs Harris came out of her house with a tin. "I've baked, too!" The two women started handing out mince pies. *I love Christmas!* Frankie thought, as he stuffed the pastry into his mouth.

"Don't you want to take off your gloves?" Mrs Harris asked as Charlie fumbled with a mince pie.

Frankie shook his head. "Can't do that," he said.

"He's got to stay ready," added Louise.

Mrs Harris looked confused.

Frankie laughed to himself. Most people didn't understand Charlie's obsession with goalkeeping.

"OK, countdown from three!" called Mr Harris. He was standing by a switch just inside his garage side-door.

Frankie joined in the count.
"*Three! Two! One!*"

Mr Harris flicked the switch and the lights all came on together. The crowd gasped. The penguins all glittered with white spots like snow crystals. The front of the house came alive with stars. Most impressive of all was the Santa on the garage. The lights were blinking

off and on along the sled, making
it appear to shoot through the air.
A red light flashed on Rudolph's
nose, and white pulses of light from
Santa's mouth looked like breath
misting on a cold night.

Everyone burst into applause.

Mr Harris folded his arms
proudly and stepped back to
admire his work. Then he frowned.
The tallest penguin hadn't lit up.
He jogged across the garden,
lifted its wing, and pressed a
hidden button. Instantly, the
penguin's eyes glowed orange,
and its wings waggled up and
down.

"That's fantastic, Alan," said Frankie's dad.

Mr Harris turned to them, and his eyes travelled up and down Frankie's dad's tracksuit. "Training, are you?" he said with a nasty smile. "Not for the Santa Race, I hope."

"Yes, actually," said Frankie's dad.

"Really?" said Mr Harris. "Well, I'll see you tomorrow. I've been training since June." He patted his flat stomach. "Rowing machine at 5 a.m., egg whites for breakfast, then weights and gym work in the afternoon."

Frankie's dad looked at the mince pie in his hand. "Yes, well . . ."

"Don't worry, Dad," said Frankie. "It's the taking part that counts."

Mr Harris grinned smugly. "And the winning, of course." He turned away, shaking hands with the crowd. Gradually, people began to drift away.

"See you tomorrow at the park, Frankie?" said Louise. "Better make the most of the good weather while we can."

Frankie was about to reply when he felt his football being snatched from under his arm. "Maybe I'll come and play tomorrow," said

Kevin. "Teach you lot a thing or two."

"Give it back, Kev," said Frankie. He looked around nervously. The last thing he needed was the football's magic kicking in while people were watching.

Kevin glanced past Frankie's head. "Reckon I can kick it over our roof?" he asked.

"No!" said Frankie and his friends together.

Kevin grinned, tossed the ball in the air and kicked it in a high arc towards the house. For a second, Frankie thought it would make it. But at the top of its loop,

a gust seemed to catch the ball. It bounced on to the tiles, then fell back down. With his heart in his mouth, Frankie watched the ball fall, fall, fall – right towards the penguins in Mr Harris's front garden.

Crash! The ball thumped into the largest penguin's head, knocking it over. A shower of sparks sprayed up from the fallen creature.

One by one, all the lights in the garden and across the house blinked out until Frankie was standing in pitch black.

CHAPTER 2

There was complete silence. Frankie could just see Charlie's mouth hanging open. A cold wind blew across the front of the houses, and Louise let out a "*Brrrrrr!*".

"What have you done?" screeched Mr Harris. He was standing by his model penguins, hands clutching his hair in the moonlight. "My display!" Then his

23

eyes fell on the football. "You!" he said, pointing a trembling finger at Frankie. "You've ruined everything."

"It was Kevin," said Frankie, turning to his brother.

But Kevin wasn't there. He'd run off.

Frankie's mum and dad looked at him with disappointment. "Oh, Frankie," said his mum. "You really shouldn't have been playing here by the road."

"But it wasn't—" Frankie began.

"He's shorted all the electrics!" said Mr Harris, pointing at the darkened house.

"Say sorry," Frankie's mum told him.

Frankie didn't want to. You said "sorry" if you'd done something wrong. Surely it wasn't right to lie? But everyone was staring.

"Come on, young man," said Mr Harris, glaring.

Frankie bit his tongue. "I'm sorry," he mumbled.

"You'd better go inside," said his dad. "Let me handle things with Mr Harris."

Frankie thought about arguing, but he could see it wouldn't get him anywhere. A few of the neighbours were still around and they were all looking at him, too. Anger swelled in his chest. When he got his hands on Kevin, he'd . . .

"Come on," said Louise, putting a hand on his arm. Charlie was retrieving the football.

Frankie stomped indoors, followed by his friends and Max.

"Kevin!" called Frankie.

No answer.

He went into the living room, then the kitchen. No sign of his brother. The Christmas tree sparkled. "At least *your* lights are all right," muttered Charlie.

"He must be upstairs," said Frankie.

"Maybe you should calm down a bit," said Louise. "Take a deep breath."

But Frankie wasn't in any mood to calm down. "He *knows* what the football can do, but he's always messing around with it. I've had enough!"

He ran up the stairs, and burst into Kevin's room. It was disgusting and smelly, as always, with dirty clothes all over the floor and plates of old food on the desk. His mum always said that Kevin's room was like a pigsty, but Frankie thought that was unfair to pigs.

There was no sign of Kevin.

Frankie tried the bathroom, and his parents' room, then finally his own. There was still wrapping paper and sticky tape on his bed, where he'd been wrapping his mum and dad's presents earlier. He'd even bought Kevin a new T-shirt, but now he wanted to chop it into pieces.

"He must be hiding somewhere," said Frankie.

Outside, he could hear raised voices as his dad argued with Mr Harris.

"Let's sit down," said Louise.

"I agree," said a gruff voice. "That was seriously awkward."

Everyone looked down. "Max?" said Frankie. "You're talking!"

"I suppose I am," replied the dog.

"But that means—" said Charlie.

"The football has worked its magic," interrupted Louise.

Frankie's anger seeped away, to be replaced by worry. The football normally opened up a portal that took them somewhere. Or it brought something to them. But this time, nothing seemed to have changed — apart from Max talking.

And Kevin vanishing, Frankie suddenly thought. A chill trickled down his spine. "Guys, you don't

think the football might have ...
taken Kevin somewhere, do you?"

"Nah! He's probably just lying
low," said Max.

"Don't worry about him," said
Charlie.

Frankie sank on to his bed. A
howling wind kicked up against the
window. Then, something white

drifted down from the sky and
settled against the pane. It was a
large snowflake.

"That's weird," said Louise. "It's
not cold enough to snow."

But as they watched, more flakes
scattered from above. In a matter
of seconds, snow was falling thick
and fast.

"We'd better get home," said
Louise. "Will you be all right,
Frankie?"

"I'll look after him," said Max,
jumping on to the bed and nuzzling
beside Frankie's leg.

Frankie said goodbye to his
friends. Wherever his brother was,

Frankie hoped Kevin would be ready to say sorry when he came back.

Santa Claus flew over the town in his sled. By Frankie's house the sled hovered, reindeer treading the air, as Santa took out his clipboard. On it was a list with two columns — one said "Naughty" and the other was headed "Nice". Only the children who had been good received presents. Luckily, the Nice column was always a lot longer than the Naughty one.

Santa Claus climbed down on to the roof with his sack of gifts.

Frankie was watching from his bedroom window. Santa paused and checked his list. Then he double-checked. Frankie cracked open his window and a blast of cold air made him shiver.

"That can't be right," Frankie heard Santa mutter. "Frankie's been naughty this year!"

"No, wait!" Frankie tried to call, as the sled disappeared into the night. "It was Kevin, not me! Wait! Wait . . ."

Frankie bolted up in bed, gasping.

"Are you all right?" asked Max dozily from the bottom of the duvet. "You were calling out in your sleep."

Frankie took a few deep breaths.

"I had a nightmare," he said.

He shivered. It was cold in the room. He wondered if he should go downstairs and turn the heating on. Checking his bedside clock, he saw it was midnight. His parents would be in bed for sure.

Frankie climbed out of bed, and his toes sank into the carpet. He went to his window and drew back the curtains. "Oh!" he breathed.

Outside, it was much brighter than he expected. Snow had been falling heavily all night. It looked almost a metre deep, covering gardens in a thick blanket and hiding the road completely. In places it had banked even higher against walls. The cars in the street were white lumps.

"Guess we'll have a white Christmas after all," said Max, leaning on the sill with his paws. There were icicles hanging from the top of Frankie's window frame and from the eaves of the houses opposite.

Frankie was sorry to see that Mr Harris's lights were still out. Now only the heads of the penguins were visible, the rest of their bodies hidden in the snow.

"There has to be some way I can make everything right," said Frankie.

"Call an electrician?" said Max.

Frankie glared at him for a second, but couldn't help smiling. "Not helpful, boy," he muttered.

Something moved in Mr Harris's garden. The surface of the snow shifted and creaked.

"What the ... ?" Frankie began to mutter. Then the snow cracked open, and Frankie jerked back in shock. It was a penguin's head sticking out – the one that Kevin had knocked over. The model creature scrambled out of the thick snow. It shook its black head and snow tumbled away. Its orange eyes scanned the empty road and house fronts.

But there's no electricity, Frankie thought. *How are his eyes glowing like that?*

Frankie's pulse raced as he leant closer to the window, his breath steaming the glass. He couldn't believe what he was seeing. The penguin flapped its stubby wings. Then it hopped across the lawn, but jerked to a stop as the power cable attached to its bottom tugged tight. With a little jump, the cable came loose.

But the lights stayed on. "That's impossible," said Frankie.

"Maybe it's got a battery," said Max, but he didn't sound very convinced.

The penguin turned, its eyes gleaming mischievously as it stared at Frankie in the window. Then it shuffled off through the snow.

"I don't like the look of him," said Max.

Frankie watched the penguin go, then looked at the football resting on his windowsill.

What had the magic done?

CHAPTER 3

Frankie hardly slept, unable to believe what he'd seen. But at some point he must have dropped off again, because when he woke it was morning. The window was still misted white and snow covered the ground.

Max stretched at the bottom of his bed.

"Can you still talk?" Frankie asked.

"I can always talk," said Max. "It's you who can't always understand me. Now, about breakfast . . ."

"Don't worry," said Frankie. "I'll get you some dog food in a minute."

Max shook his head. "Actually, I'd quite like some toast."

"All right," said Frankie.

"With marmalade?"

"Fine. Max, aren't you worried about that penguin? The football's brought it to life."

"What harm can a penguin do?" said Max. "They can't even fly!"

Frankie padded downstairs in his football pyjamas.

"Morning," said Frankie. He could hardly look either of his parents in the eye after the night before.

"Morning, love," said his mum. "Do you want some breakfast?"

Max made a little yapping sound, pawing at Frankie's leg.

"Could I have some toast, please?" said Frankie. "With marmalade."

As his mum put the bread in the toaster, Frankie looked into his back garden. Like the rest of the neighbourhood, it was under a heavy blanket of snow.

The phone rang, and Frankie's dad picked it up. "Hello?"

Frankie saw his dad's face fall. "Really?" he said. "But ... Yes, I understand ... OK, bye Pete." He put the phone down slowly.

"What's the matter?" asked Frankie's mum.

His dad shrugged. "The Santa Race – they're saying they'll have to cancel because of the snow. Health and safety, apparently. It's not going to melt by this afternoon."

"No!" said Frankie's mum. "You trained so hard, sweetheart."

Frankie saw his dad's glance travel to his bright red Santa suit, hanging on the back of the door.

His trainers, scrubbed clean, sat on the floor beneath the suit.

Frankie munched on his toast, feeding bits to Max under the table. The weather had been so mild yesterday. Now, there'd been an overnight snowstorm and Max was talking. *This is all because of the magic football.* Frankie felt sure of it. He needed to find Louise and Charlie. He might be able to fix this, but only with his teammates.

"I'm going out," he said.

His mum and dad looked at each other. "Just stay away from Mr Harris," said his dad. "He's fuming after last night."

Frankie went to his room and dressed for the cold weather, pulling on thick socks and several layers. At the back of his drawers he found a scarf, hat and gloves. From the shoe cupboard downstairs he grabbed his trainers. Max was following him around, ready to leave.

When he opened the door, Charlie and Louise were on his doorstep.

"We need to talk," said Louise, her breath misting the air. "Something's not right."

"I know," whispered Frankie. "I saw something really weird last night."

Frankie stepped outside and closed the door behind him. Both his friends were dressed in thick coats. Charlie was wearing a checked hat and Louise had ear-muffs. Snow reached their ankles. Max leapt into the nearest drift and sank without a trace.

Frankie leant down and pulled him out, white powder caking his fur.

"What did you see?" Louise asked. Frankie told them about the penguin that had climbed out of the snow, eyes glowing. The giant penguin that had wandered off into town.

"Are you sure?" asked Charlie.

"Come with me," said Frankie.

They trudged away from the house towards Mr Harris's front garden. Frankie pointed to the humps where the penguins were concealed. "Look, there are only three now. There were four yesterday. The one the football hit has run off!"

As they approached, Frankie saw the snow was still disturbed where the penguin had broken loose from the cable. "Footprints," said Charlie, peering closer.

Frankie saw he was right. Large, three-pronged marks trailed across the snow. "Let's follow them!"

"Get off my lawn!" shouted a voice. "And take that football with you!"

They looked up to see Mr Harris leaning out of a window.

Frankie and his friends ran off as quickly as they could through the snow. Soon they reached the park. The penguin's tracks led right through the gates. "I wonder where he's heading," said Frankie. "It's like he knows where he's going."

He'd never seen the park look so spooky. All the swings and slides were coated with icicles. The lines that marked the football pitches had vanished under the white cloak of snow. Max charged ahead, kicking up white powder.

The footprints headed for the lake at the bottom of the park.

Frankie quickened his steps, trudging through the snowfall.

Charlie was panting to keep up at his side. When they reached the raised bank of the lake, Frankie gasped. The whole lake was covered in ice. Everyone knew that the lake in this park never froze over! Lying in the centre, wings tucked behind his head, was the penguin.

"Er . . . hello!" shouted Frankie, looking around. Fortunately, no one else seemed to be in the park. He wouldn't like anyone other than his friends to see him talking to a giant penguin!

Max barked furiously.

The penguin wobbled on to its

feet, and cocked its head. Then, gliding like an ice-skater, it sailed towards them across the frozen surface. It approached them faster and faster, until Frankie thought there was no way it could stop. But at the last moment, it turned, and swept past in an arc.

"Lovely day, isn't it?" the penguin called back over its shoulder.

Lovely? Frankie had never felt so cold in his life.

"Not really," said Charlie, shivering hard.

"Who are you?" yelled Louise.

The penguin suddenly twisted and stopped dead.

"I am Emperor Frostie," he said. The penguin gave a bow, then carried on skating.

"Er, hello, Mr Frostie," Frankie said.

"*Emperor* Frostie," the penguin said. "And who are you?"

"I'm Frankie," he said. "You came from my neighbour's garden."

The penguin raised his beak. "I assure you I did not. I'm from the North Pole."

"Penguins are from the South Pole," said Louise in a quiet voice. Frankie looked at his friends. This all felt really wrong.

Frostie's eyes narrowed.

"Whatever. I'm here now, just in time."

"Just in time for what?" asked Frankie, as snow started to fall.

The penguin looked at him hard. "In time to create the winter that never ends," he said, folding his wings in front of him. "Happy Christmas!"

CHAPTER 4

"A winter that never ends?" said Frankie.

"Yes. You know what 'for ever' means, don't you?" said the penguin.

Frankie glanced at his friends, then back at the skating penguin. "But . . . you can't!"

Frostie shrugged. "I already have. This town is just the start. My winter will spread all around the world by nightfall."

"How can you?" said Frankie. "They've already had to cancel the Santa Race. If this snow doesn't clear up, people won't be able to visit their families for Christmas."

"Christmas!" said Frostie, in a tone of disgust. "The only thing I like about Christmas is the mince pies. Santa cast a spell over me and tried to keep me away, but that magic football has woken me up." He swerved past in a loop the loop.

"Oh, great!" said Charlie. "It *was* Kevin's fault!"

"It's a shame your brother isn't here to thank," Frostie called over his shoulder.

Frankie's blood ran cold. "What do you mean?"

"I passed the curse on," said the penguin. "Well, the ball did, somehow."

Frankie struggled to understand. Then he thought back to Kevin's empty bed that morning.

"What have you done to him?" he demanded.

Frostie's beak became a wicked grin. "Wouldn't you like to know?"

Frankie laid a foot cautiously on the ice. Frostie slid backwards, further towards the middle of the lake.

"Careful, Frankie," said Louise.

Frankie took another step. The ice seemed firm. Max scampered beside him.

"Where is my brother?" said Frankie.

The penguin was only a few metres away. *If I can just grab him, get him to understand how important this is.* The penguin had to tell him where Kevin was. He might be a horrible brother sometimes, but Frankie didn't want him to miss Christmas.

He shuffled forward. The ice

gave a horrible creak, and Frankie felt it shift a little under his feet. Then it began to change colour, becoming darker. He realised he was seeing the water beneath. The ice was getting thinner!

Frostie cackled. "Ready for a cold bath?"

"Run, Frankie!" called Louise. "Get off the ice!"

They started to run. Frankie scooped up Max and staggered back towards the bank, as cracks spread out across the lake. As he jumped, the surface gave way and freezing water swallowed one foot, flooding his trainer. He tossed Max to dry land and managed to drag himself back on to the bank. When he stood up, he saw the penguin on an island of ice in the centre of the lake, far out of reach.

Frankie glowered – he couldn't even feel his foot. He took off his shoe and tipped the water out.

"Come on," he said to his friends. "I've got a plan."

"You have?" said Louise.

Frankie nodded grimly. "We need the magic football. If it brought Frostie here, it can send him back again. But first, we need to find Kevin."

By the time they got home, more snow was falling, and Frankie's wet sock had frozen solid.

But Frankie could only think about Kevin. What was he going to tell his mum and dad?

"It's all right," said Louise, placing a hand on his shoulder. "We'll get him back ... somehow."

Mr Harris was in his front

garden, digging out his model penguins. Frankie wondered how long it would be before he noticed one was missing.

As Frankie opened the front door, the smell of baking filled his nostrils. Max whined hungrily.

"Mince pies!" said Charlie. "Yum!"

"Focus," said Frankie. "We need to work out what's happened to my brother."

"Back already, you three!" said Frankie's mum. "Isn't Kevin with you?"

"Er ..." Frankie hated lying to his parents, but while there was a chance he could fix this, he didn't want to frighten them. "He was out, looking for a present for Nan," he said. "He got up early."

His dad's eyebrows shot up. "Well, there's a first time for everything." He pointed to the tray of mince pies. "Hungry?"

Frankie's mum swatted him with an oven glove. "Don't be cheeky."

Max's nose twitched, and his head jerked towards the living room. He pawed at Frankie's foot and trotted out of the kitchen.

Charlie was already reaching for a mince pie.

"I'll have one in a minute," said

Frankie, following Max. Louise came too, dragging Charlie with her. Frankie shut the door behind them. "What's up, boy?"

"I can smell him!" growled Max. "Kevin. The stink is unmistakable."

Frankie looked around the living room. Unless he was hiding behind the sofa, Kevin wasn't here. Max's snout went to the ground, and he trotted towards the Christmas tree. Mum didn't normally like him going near it, after one year when he'd tried to grab a decoration and pulled the whole thing down.

He sniffed around the base

of the tree, then lifted his nose. Suddenly he stopped completely still.

"Oh dear," he said. "You might want to have a look at this."

Frankie rushed over and crouched beside his pet. At first he couldn't see anything unusual. He'd helped decorate the tree this year, hanging baubles, and tinsel, and little model owls and robins.

But then his eyes settled on one decoration that looked slightly out of place, not Christmassy at all. It was a figurine of a boy, dressed in a pair of jeans and a hooded top. Frankie felt sick.

"It can't be . . ." he said, reaching out. Gently, he plucked the model off a branch.

"How am I going to get Kevin back for Christmas?" Frankie muttered, turning the tiny boy over in his hands.

Frankie's brother had turned into a tree decoration! He looked up at his friends. Had the magic football ruined Christmas for good?

PART TWO

CHAPTER 5

"Kev?" whispered Frankie. "Is that
you?"

Kevin's face was set in a scowl.
It looked like he really, really didn't
like being a Christmas decoration.

"Everything all right in here?"
said Frankie's mum. "You're all very
quiet."

Frankie quickly shoved the
figurine behind his back.

"Yeah ... fine!" he said.

"I hope you're not pinching chocolates off the tree," said his mum, smiling. "Not until after Christmas Day, remember."

Frankie could feel the blush rising to his cheeks. "Of course not," he said.

His mum headed back into the kitchen, leaving Frankie and his friends alone.

He cradled Kevin in his hands for them all to see. "Frostie has turned him into a useless piece of plastic!" he said.

"I can't really tell the difference," said Max, with a snigger.

"This isn't funny," said Frankie. "We've got to make Frostie turn Kevin into a real boy again."

"How?" said Charlie.

Frankie didn't answer, but ran up the stairs to his bedroom. He put on clean socks and grabbed his football from the windowsill. It didn't look magical at all – just scuffed and dirty. But he knew it had the power to send Frostie back where he came from. After he'd helped get Kevin back.

His friends were waiting downstairs.

"Going out again?" asked his mum, who was standing in the hallway with a tray. "Don't you want a mince pie first? Go on, Charlie, take a few."

"Don't mind if I do," said Charlie, scooping them up in his gloves and popping them in his coat pocket.

Frankie couldn't find his appetite. His fingers touched the figure in his pocket.

I won't let my brother down.

The park was busier when they returned. A few kids were out with sledges, or building snowmen and having snowball fights. Everyone was making the most of this sudden white Christmas. There was no sign of Frostie.

"Great! He's gone," said Charlie. "What now?"

Just as Frankie was losing hope, he saw bubbles forming underneath the ice on the lake, rising up from the water below. A shape shot beneath the water, quick as a torpedo, and a second later burst through the ice. Frostie slid along the bank then wobbled upright. He shook the water from his feathers.

Frankie pulled Kevin from his pocket and dangled him. "Turn my brother back!" he said. Fortunately, all the other people in the park were too busy playing to notice that he was talking to a penguin!

Frostie laughed softly. "I can't do that, I'm afraid."

"Why not?" said Frankie.

"Because if I help him get back to normal, I'll go back under the spell," said the penguin. "I'm not ready to do that yet. I have a horrible winter to spread. Remember?"

How could Frankie forget?
He felt the football tingle a little beneath his arm. The magic football had brought Frostie to life – it must have the power to reverse the process. He slipped Kevin back into his pocket and held the ball in both hands.

Frostie's eyes widened and he

flapped his wings. "Don't come near me with that thing!" he said.

I knew it, thought Frankie. *He's scared.*

"Spread out," he whispered to his friends. "Surround him."

Louise went one way, Charlie the other. "Oh no, you don't," said Frostie. He turned and waddled away quickly across the snow.

"After him!" cried Max, causing a small boy on a sled to look round in shock.

They all chased the penguin. With his webbed feet, Frostie was quick, sliding across the surface of the snow. Frankie struggled, feet

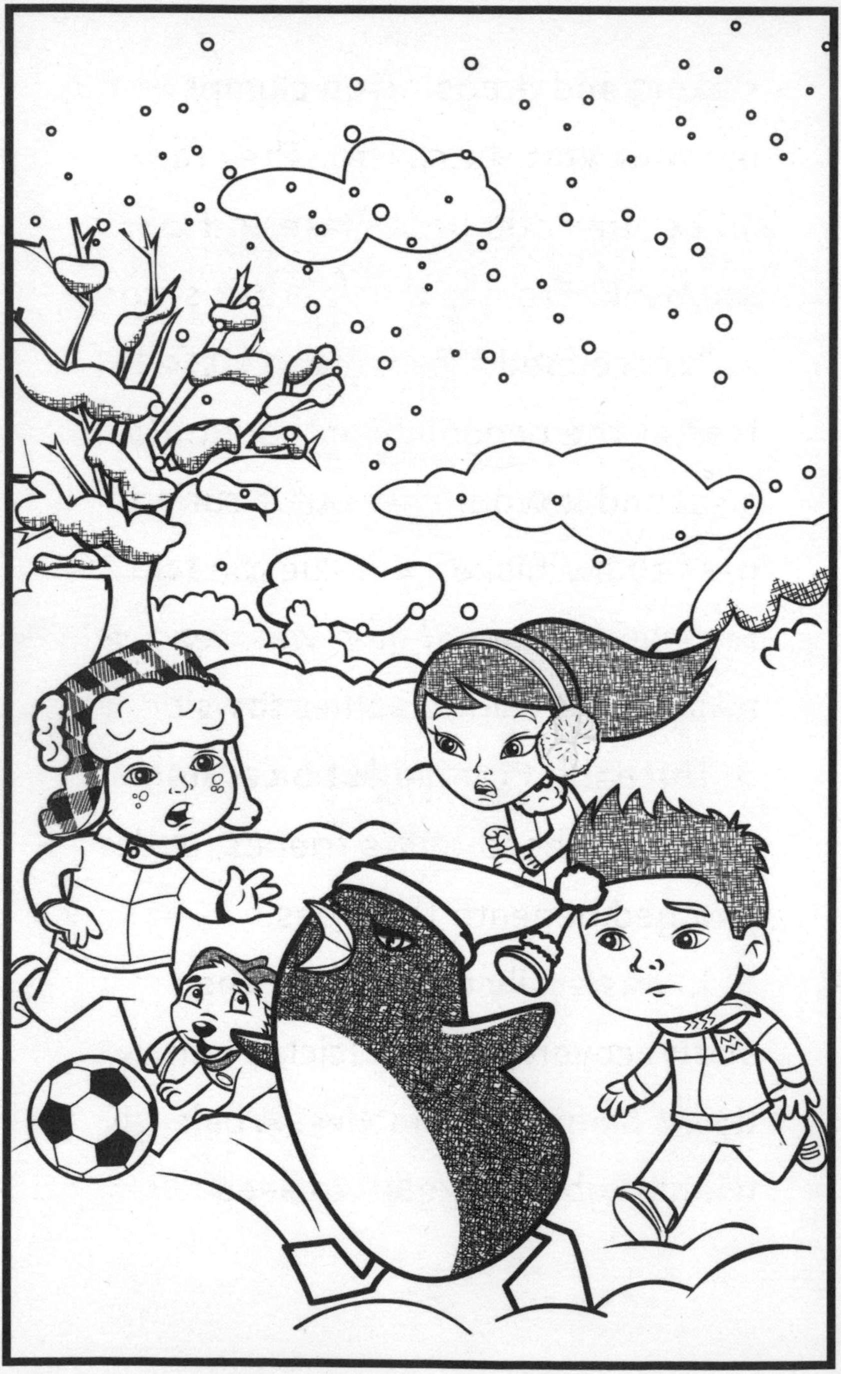

sinking and dragging up clumps
of snow with each step. They ran
along the edge of the lake and up
the bank. Frankie didn't break stride
as he dropped the ball, and kicked
it after the penguin. He thought for
a second it would hit, but it curled
past by a whisker. Frankie ran to
retrieve it. The penguin was heading
towards the woodland at the side
of the park. Frankie put on a burst
of speed ahead of his friends, and
plunged beneath the trees.

It was eerily quiet under the
snow-covered trees. Icicles hung
down from the branches. A pale
wintry light struggled to seep

through, casting shadows across the ground. There were no birds, so the only sound was the crunch of Frankie's footsteps.

"Come out!" he called. "You can't run for ever, Frostie."

"*Emperor* Frostie," came the reply. The voice echoed around the trees, seeming to come from all directions at once. It was impossible to know where his enemy was hiding.

Frankie stepped forwards. He could hear his friends shuffling between the trees too. The wood wasn't large and a fence surrounded it on three sides.

Gradually they would close in on the penguin.

He heard a strange cracking sound above.

"Look out!" cried Charlie.

As Frankie glanced up, he saw a large, pointed icicle falling through the air, right towards him. The next moment something barreled into his side. It was Charlie, and they crashed down together in the snow. The icicle stood upright in the ground, gleaming, right where Frankie had been standing.

"Thanks!" he said to Charlie. "You saved me."

"You know me — always ready!"

said Charlie, patting his goalie
gloves together.

Louise and Max arrived at their
side. "Are you OK?" Louise asked,
her face pale.

"Frostie is sneaky," said Frankie.
"Let's watch out."

They stood up, dusting off the snow. Just then, Frostie dropped down from a branch and stepped out in front of them. Frankie dropped the ball, ready to take a shot.

"You dodged one icicle," said the penguin. "Let's see how you cope with a few more."

He opened his beak in a series of high-pitched squeaks, as a cold wind swept through the wood. Branches trembled, trickling powdery snow. The icicles twinkled, and there was a snapping noise as several of them fell towards the ground. Louise jumped back, just dodging an icicle as it plunged into the snow.

"I think we'd better get out of here," said Louise, as icicles fell all around them. She and Frankie raced between trees, swerving to avoid the falling icicles. It was like running through an obstacle course – only with more chance of getting really hurt. Max pulled ahead, towards the edge of the wood. Eventually, they burst out into a clearing. Frankie's lungs hurt from gasping in cold air. He swiveled round, ready to thank Charlie again for helping him. Frankie looked from Louise, to Max, to . . .

Now, it really did feel like ice had plunged into his heart.

"Where's Charlie?" he asked, peering back into the wood. Their friend had disappeared!

CHAPTER 6

"Charlie!" Frankie called, panic rising in his chest.

"Where are you?" shouted Louise.

Max sniffed the air. "This way!" he barked, running off through the trees.

Soon, Frankie saw a gloved hand sticking up through a small mound of snow. Max set about digging with his front paws, and Frankie joined him with Louise, heaving lumps of snow off their friend. Charlie wriggled free. His lips were blue, and his teeth were chattering.

"Th ... th ... thanks, guys," he stuttered.

Frankie looked around. With the branches of the trees bare, there was more light in the wood. "Where's that penguin hiding now?" he said.

Charlie's eyes lit up. "I've got an idea," he said. From his pocket, he pulled out two of the mince pies.

"That's not very helpful," said Max. "There'll be time to eat later."

"No, listen," said Charlie.
"Remember what Frostie said?
The only thing he likes about
Christmas is the mince pies.
Maybe we can tempt him out using
these ones."

"It's got to be worth a try," said
Louise.

"Good thinking," said Frankie.
"There's a clearing just through the
trees — let's lay a trail. If we can
get him in the open, I'll have a clear
shot."

Charlie broke off a piece of
the pastry and scattered it on the
ground. They walked a few paces,
then did the same again.

"Come on, let's go home!" said
Frankie loudly, hoping Frostie could
hear. "We'll never find him."

They laid pieces of mince pie
all the way to the clearing in the
middle of the wood. In the centre,
Charlie put down a whole one.
Frankie pointed to some trees on

the far edge, and they all took up positions behind the trunks.

I hope this works, thought Frankie. *All we can do is wait.*

It didn't take long. At first Frankie just heard the shuffle of steps, then Frostie appeared between the trees, stooping every few steps to peck at the ground, before tossing back his head and swallowing the pieces of mince pie.

"Yummy, yummy!" the penguin muttered as he swallowed greedily, flakes of pastry falling down his front.

Frankie placed the football carefully on the ground. He knew he'd only get one shot, just like a penalty. He had to make it count.

At the edge of the clearing, Frostie paused with crumbs on his beak. He'd spotted the mince pie right in the middle of the clearing. He looked around suspiciously. Had he guessed what their plan was?

Come on, thought Frankie, holding his breath. *Step into the open.*

Eventually, the penguin began to waddle into the clearing, stopping every few paces to look around. He was being really careful, but his love of mince pies was getting the better of him. Frankie had never been so grateful for his mum's baking! From behind a tree, Louise gave Frankie a thumbs-up. Charlie mouthed, "Now!"

Frankie waited. Frostie was edging towards the mince pie. The best time to try to kick the ball at him would be as he bent over.

The penguin suddenly marched into the centre of the clearing. Glancing quickly around, he lowered his head.

Frankie jumped out and kicked the ball. It was a perfect shot, straight and low, and it struck Frostie on the head, bouncing away. He looked up, beak full of pastry crumbs.

"Ha!" said Frostie. "Did you think it would be that easy to send me back under the spell?" He picked Frankie's ball up under a wing. "The magic isn't strong enough, I'm afraid."

How could that be? The football's magic had always worked. But now Frankie could see that a thick frost was covering the leather panels. Was the cold affecting the football, too?

"You don't really want to get rid of me, do you?" asked the penguin in a mocking voice.

Frankie's whole body was

shivering now. "I just want my brother back."

"I never thought I'd hear you say that!" whispered Charlie, patting his gloved hands together for warmth.

The penguin's eyes narrowed. "How touching," he said. "But you lose, I'm afraid."

Something inside Frankie sparked into life. He'd hardly ever lost a game, and he wasn't about to start now.

"Are you sure about that?" he called over. He began walking towards the penguin and took the ball back, turning it over in his hands. "I bet I'd win against you," he said.

The penguin's face hardened. "Never!"

Frankie's plan was working. He could see that he was tempting his enemy into a game.

"You couldn't win a game of football with those things," he said, pointing to the penguin's stubby feet.

"I've never seen a penguin score a goal ever in my life," added Louise, coming up behind Frankie.

Charlie was still clapping his goalie gloves together. "I wouldn't even have to try to stop a goal," he said. "You wouldn't be able to score one!"

"Enough!" cried the penguin. "Let's play."

"You don't even have a team," said Max.

Frostie grinned and let out a squawk. All around him, the snow broke apart and three penguins' heads emerged.

"They're the other models from the garden," Frankie said. All three started stretching.

"If we win, you bring my brother back," Frankie said.

Frostie laughed. "And if you lose, your brother stays as he is for ever. *Plus* I get to keep the ball."

"No way," said Charlie.

Frankie glanced at his friends. "We don't have a choice," he said. He turned to the penguin. "How can we trust you to keep your word?"

Frostie ruffled his feathers, looking offended. "I always keep my promises," he said. "It's my biggest weakness, after mince pies.

Score a goal against Frostie FC, and your brother will be returned, good as new."

"And you'll go back to wherever you came from?" said Frankie.

"Emperor's honour," said Frostie, saluting with his wing-tip.

Frankie nodded. He had a feeling their enemy would have a trick or two under his wings, but they had to give this a try.

"Let's play," he said.

CHAPTER 7

They took their positions either side of the clearing. Frostie went in goal for his team, between two trees, and his three penguin teammates lined up in front of him. *They look like a tough defence*, thought Frankie.

He kicked the ball to Louise, but because of the thick snow it didn't go far. One of Frostie's team slid

on its belly to the ball, and used its
beak to guide it. Max scampered into
its path, but the penguin dodged
easily around him. Louise trudged
through the snow and lunged with
a foot. She managed the tackle, but
she was bogged down and the ball

ran free. As Frankie threw himself after it, another penguin got there much quicker and shot towards goal. Charlie caught it perfectly.

"Come on, guys," he said. "We can't let them win!"

He tossed the ball to Max's feet. In front of the goal, the three penguins suddenly dived, burrowing into the snow.

Frostie laughed. "Come on, it's an open goal!"

Max, tongue lolling, ran with the ball, controlling it with his little legs. Louise and Frankie struggled alongside him. When they were five metres out, Max nosed the ball to

Frankie. He lifted his foot to shoot, but at the same time a penguin burst out of the ground in front of him, knocking the ball away. Frankie swung his foot, lost his balance and landed on his back in the freezing snow.

He glanced back in desperation and saw the penguins heading for Charlie's goal again. It was three on one. *They're in their element,* Frankie thought.

"It's all over!" gloated Frostie.

But Charlie had other plans. He reached into his pocket and pulled out another mince pie. "Here, you lot!" he shouted, and tossed it into the air. The penguins forgot about the ball and all leapt up, fighting over the mince pie.

"You fools!" called Frostie, as Charlie scooped up the ball.

He quickly rolled it across the snow towards Louise, but it hit a clump of snow and veered off-path. Louise stretched out a foot and managed to connect, just. The ball flew in a looping arc over Max's head. Frankie bounded towards it, each step in the deep snow sapping his strength. He wasn't going to make it.

"Go, Frankie!" roared Charlie.

As the ball started to drop,

Frankie summoned all his strength and dived towards the goal. He closed his eyes and flicked his head. Making contact with the ball, he fell into the snow, but he heard Louise cry out, "Supergoal!"

Frankie spat out a mouthful of snow and rose on to his hands and knees. Frostie was squatting in his goal, looking cross. "What sort of a team do you call yourself!" he shouted at his penguins. They were still pecking away at the scraps of pastry near Charlie's goal.

"Great idea, Charlie!" said Louise. "I thought we'd lost there."

Charlie looked a bit glum. "That was my last mince pie," he said.

"Hey!" said Max. "Where's he going?"

Frankie spun around. Frostie was making off from the clearing, carrying the football with him.

"Wait!" said Frankie. "You promised."

The penguin turned around. "I lied," he said with a sneer.

At that moment, under his wing, the battered leather football began to glow. Trails of golden light like tinsel wrapped around Frostie. His gleaming orange eyes widened. The sparkling strands spread from the penguin into the surrounding trees like magical creepers.

"No! What's happening?" the penguin cried. "Make it stop!"

But the sparkles only grew stronger. The football's magic was coming back!

The gold sheen spread over the penguin's body, covering him completely. He dropped the ball in panic and began to waddle away, wrapped in a golden glow, but his limbs looked stiff and slow. Frankie ran after him. By the time he reached the penguin's side, tiny crystals of white ice bristled across Frostie's feathers and wings, then his beak. He was halfway through a stride when he froze and toppled forward into the snow.

Frankie ran over to him, and turned him over. The orange light was gone from his eyes, and his beak was closed. He was just a model penguin again.

Looking back to the clearing, Frankie saw the other penguins were lying on the ground, motionless, too.

"We did it!" said Louise. "We won!"

"The football did it," said Charlie. "Hurray for Christmas!"

Frankie plunged a hand into his pocket, thinking of his brother. His fingers closed on nothing. "Oh no!" he said. "Where's Kevin?"

He checked his other pocket, just in case. Louise and Charlie looked worried too. *What had Frostie done now? What if the curse wasn't lifted?*

"You might have dropped him," said Louise.

Frankie thought of their mad dash through the wood, and when Charlie had pushed him out of the icicle's path. "We need to retrace our steps. Max, keep your nose peeled."

His pet dog gave a determined bark. Frankie guessed he couldn't speak any longer, now that everything was back to normal. Well, almost everything.

CHAPTER 8

As they set off back through the trees towards the park, the snow began melting – fast. Frankie could feel the air warming up. Patches of grass began to appear. What little snow remained on the tree branches dripped off, sending cold trickles over their heads and down their collars. Frankie realised he could no longer see his breath on the air, and he began to sweat inside his thick coat. The winter spell was lifting.

But where was Kevin?

At the edge of the wood, they looked out across the park. The snow was gone here too, and snowmen were sinking into the ground before their eyes, leaving an assortment of scarves, carrot-noses and woolly hats lying on the slushy ground. Kids and parents watched in astonishment, then began to drag their useless sleds towards the park gates.

By the lake, sitting in a shrinking clump of snow, was Kevin. He looked very confused, and very wet.

"What's going on?" he said, when
he saw Frankie approaching. "I had
the strangest dream . . ."

Despite all the problems Kevin
had caused, Frankie felt sorry for
his brother. He offered a hand to
help him up. "You almost caused

a never-ending winter. Christmas was nearly ruined!"

Kevin blushed as he climbed to his feet. "I'm sorry, Frankenstein. The last thing I remember is watching Horrid Harris's light display."

"Speaking of which, we need to take Frostie and his pals back to the garden!" said Louise.

"Who's Frostie?" asked Kevin.

"It's a long story," said Frankie, "but the lesson is never to mess around with my football!"

They all told Kevin the tale as they headed back into the trees to fetch the model penguins. He laughed at the bit where Frankie got blamed for the ball incident, but he shuddered when they told him about how he'd been a decoration hanging from the tree.

"What if you hadn't found me?" he said. "Mum would have put me back in the box in the attic for a whole year!"

They found the penguins where they'd left them. Frankie shouldered Frostie, and Louise, Charlie and Kevin took another penguin each.

"We'd better hurry," said Frankie. "If Mr Harris notices they've gone, he'll be mad."

Luckily the park was pretty much empty now that the snow had melted, and they took the back streets home. It was a longer route, but no one stopped them. When they reached Frankie's road, he began to worry. What if Mr Harris was waiting?

But it looked quiet. "Quick!" said Frankie. "Before anyone sees."

They ran along the pavement and placed the model penguins back in the garden. There was no snow at all now. They'd just plugged the cables back in when Mr Harris's front door opened. Frankie's heart skipped a beat.

It was only Mrs Harris, however. She was dressed in her coat, ready to go out.

"Hello, kids," she said, smiling. "Why aren't you at the park with everyone else?"

Frankie frowned. "We were just there a few minutes ago. Why, what's going on?"

"The Santa Race, of course. It's back on! Your mum was looking for you."

Frankie glanced at his friends. He couldn't miss his dad's big race!

"Come on, I'll give you a lift," said Mrs Harris.

They all squeezed into her car,

with Max in the boot, and Mrs Harris drove off through the slushy snow.

In no time they were back at the park. As Mrs Harris found a spot for the car, Kevin cleared his throat in the front seat. "Mrs H, there's something I need to say."

"Yes, Kevin?" she replied.

"Last night," said Kevin, "it was me who kicked the football into your garden. Not Frankie. He shouldn't get the blame."

Frankie was astonished, and judging from the looks on Charlie and Louise's faces, they were just as shocked.

"That's all right, young man,"

said Mrs Harris. "Alan won't hold a grudge, I'm sure."

They all climbed out and made their way to the gates. Frankie could already see the race under way on the far side of the park. A bunch of about fifty people were huffing and puffing, all wearing Santa suits and bushy white beards. It was impossible to tell from this distance who was who.

The finish line had been erected beside the bandstand and a crowd had gathered there, including Frankie's mum.

"Thanks for owning up, Kev," said Frankie as they wandered over.

"No problem," said his brother. "Anyway, I forgot to buy you a Christmas present, so I felt guilty."

Frankie saw Louise roll her eyes and grinned. He didn't mind about the present. *Typical Kev.*

So far, most of the Santas were still together, but two had pulled ahead, running fast side by side. Frankie recognized the trainers of the one on the right. "It's Dad!" he yelled.

"Go on, Alan!" yelled Mrs Harris beside him.

As the runners rounded the final bend, Frankie realised it was Mr Harris neck and neck with his dad.

Both were puffing hard. Mr Harris threw a glance over at Frankie's dad.

"You can do it!" shouted Frankie.

Then Mr Harris stumbled. He tried to regain his balance, but he was already falling. He landed on his hands and knees and the crowd gasped.

Frankie's dad kept running, looking back over his shoulder, then slowed and stopped.

"What's he doing?" said Kevin. "The race is his for the taking!"

Frankie's dad ran back towards Mr Harris as the other Santas streamed past towards the finish line. Frankie lost sight of him behind the pack.

People cheered as the first Santa crossed the line with his arms aloft. The man was quite large but fast on his feet, and he'd made a real effort with his costume. It didn't look like one of the cheap outfits the other runners were wearing.

"He's not even wearing trainers!" said Louise, pointing to the man's heavy black boots.

A second runner staggered over the line and tugged off his fake beard. Frankie saw it was Mr Donald, their PE teacher. Everyone clapped him on the back.

"Nice one, Donaldo!" shouted Charlie.

Looking back, Frankie saw his dad helping Mr Harris towards the line as other runners streamed past. Mr Harris was limping gingerly on one ankle, with his arm over Frankie's dad's shoulder. They crossed the line together, in joint last place.

They got the loudest cheer of all.

"Well done, Dad!" said Frankie. He felt really proud of what his dad had done. An official came to hang Santa-shaped medals around their necks.

Mr Harris hugged his wife, and then turned to Frankie's dad. "That was good of you," he said. "Very sporting."

"Well, it's not all about coming first," said Frankie's dad.

They shook hands.

"I'm just glad the snow cleared up," said Frankie's dad, looking around. "I've never known such a sudden cold snap, then just as quickly ..." His voice faded away to nothing as he shook his head.

"Can I have everyone's attention for the medal ceremony?" called the race official. The crowd shifted and Frankie saw a pedestal set up,

with three steps at three heights.
Mr Donald took his place on the
second tier, stretching, and the
school lollipop lady, Mrs Peters,
stood on the bronze metal step.
She was glugging from a bottle of
water.

"She's about eighty!" whispered
Charlie.

"She once tried out for the
Olympics, apparently," muttered
Louise.

"And where's our winner?" said
the official.

"Just coming!" said a gruff voice.
The Santa wearing heavy boots
struggled up into position. He was

eating a mince pie, with crumbs scattered down his red coat.

As the gold medal was looped over his head, everyone cheered. Then Mr Donald leant towards him. "That beard could almost be real," he said. *Yes*, Frankie thought, narrowing his eyes. *It really could.*

"Thank you," the man said, dipping his head.

"Do you live locally?" asked Mrs Peters.

"Er ... no," said the winner of the Great Santa Race. His cheeks blushed above his beard. "A little north of here. Actually, I should be getting home. Long day of work ahead."

"You're working on Christmas Eve?" said Frankie's dad.

The man climbed down from the podium. Frankie noticed that he was avoiding looking at anyone.

"Excuse me," Frankie called, as the Santa began to walk away. His whole body was tingling as an idea occurred to him.

The man froze on the spot at the sound of Frankie's voice. Slowly, he turned round to meet Frankie's eye. There was definitely something familiar about this particular Santa.

His glance dropped to the football Frankie was still gripping. "You'd better keep a tight hold of that," he said, eyes twinkling. "No more adventures for now."

How does he know about our adventures? But Frankie already knew the answer to his question. "You're the real Santa, aren't you?" said Frankie, keeping his voice low.

"Maybe," came a whisper back. He reached into his pocket and pulled out another mince pie.

Max hopped up, resting his paws on the man's leg. He whimpered hopefully.

"Not for you, boy," said Santa, stroking Max's head. "I've got eight hungry reindeer to feed."

"What are their names?" Louise asked, but Santa was already walking away. Frankie quickly lost sight of him among all the other men in red suits. Charlie nudged Frankie, but before they could talk about what had happened, Frankie's parents came to his side.

"Maybe you'll get a new ball for Christmas," said his mum, draping an arm around his shoulders.

"Yeah, that one is a bit . . ." said Frankie's dad.

"Unpredictable?" said Louise.

"I was going to say 'tatty'," said his dad, as they all headed back to Frankie's house.

Frankie thought of all the adventures the magic football had taken them on. OK, so occasionally it got them into trouble, but they always came out on top! Their football had helped teach Kevin not to cause trouble and Frankie had even had an apology from his older brother. This was the best Christmas of all!

"I think I'll stick with this one," he said, hugging the ball to his chest. Santa was right. He'd need to keep it safe until Christmas was over. But after that? Who knew what adventures it would lead to next!

ACKNOWLEDGEMENTS

Many thanks to everyone at Hachette Children's Group; Neil Blair, Zoe King, Daniel Teweles and all at The Blair Partnership; Luella Wright for bringing my characters to life; special thanks to Michael Ford for all his wisdom and patience; and to Steve Kutner for being a great friend and for all his help and guidance, not just with the book but with everything.

Turn the page for
an exclusive extract
from Frankie's next
adventure, *Team T-Rex*,

coming soon!

*Frankie and his friends
are at a closed-down
theme park ...*

The Galaxy Quest ride was silent.
Frankie peered at the other
attractions. There was a ghost
house, a huge part-deflated
bouncy castle, and something
called Under the Sea. But his
eyes fell on a roller coaster called
T-Rex Runaway. It threaded

between fake boulders and volcanoes, under rainforest trees. Pretend dinosaurs loomed over the track.

He saw Charlie was looking at the same thing. "Let's try that one!" he said.

"Are you sure?" said Louise. "It might be dangerous."

"The football has always kept us safe before," said Frankie.

Louise nodded, and they all scrambled into the coaster cart, and pulled down the safety bars. Max sat in Frankie's lap.

Nothing happened.

Frankie looked at the football

between his feet. "Oh," he said. "I thought—"

A hissing sound interrupted him and the cart jerked forward. The football sparkled.

"It's working!" said Charlie. "Hang on, everyone!"

Frankie's back pressed against the seat as the cart rattled up the track. Glancing over the edge, it looked much higher than it had seemed on the ground. A ball of nerves was building in his gut. Louise's knuckles were white where they gripped the safety bar. Max had flattened his ears.

They reached the highest point,

and over the wall of the theme park Frankie could see the holiday camp stretching out. He worried for a moment that people might see them, but then the cart began to tip forward slowly.

"Woo-hoo!" yelled Charlie as they plummeted down the other side. Frankie felt the wind dragging against his cheeks and his heart thumped in his chest. The cart shot down the slope, then leaned to one side as the track entered a turn. It climbed again up a loop, and Frankie lost his bearings as it turned upside-down. For a second he was

weightless, then they zoomed
down the other side.

This is awesome! he thought.

He saw a huge model dinosaur
head in front of them, as big as
a van. Its mouth gaped, revealing
dagger-like teeth. The track went
straight through its open jaws
and into the dark tunnel beyond.
Frankie pushed himself against
the seat and they all screamed as
the cart headed into the unknown.

But as they entered the
darkness, the rattling stopped,
as if the cart had left the track
completely. Frankie felt suddenly
weightless, as if they were

zooming through the air. Frankie saw light ahead — the end of the tunnel. It grew as they flew towards it. Frankie made out a rocky fringe, and green plants beyond. The cart soared out into the open then fell towards the ground in some sort of forest.

"We're going to crash!" cried Louise.

Competition Time

COULD YOU BE A WINNER LIKE FRANKIE?

Every month one lucky fan will win an exclusive
Frankie's Magic Football goodie bag! Here's how to enter:

Every **Frankie's Magic Football** book
features different animals. Go to:
www.frankiesmagicfootball.co.uk/competitions
and name three different animals that feature in three
different **Frankie's Magic Football** books.
Then you could be a winner!

You can also send your entry by post by filling in
the form on the opposite page.

Once complete, please send your entries to:

Frankie's Magic Football Competition
Hachette Children's Books, Carmelite House,
50 Victoria Embankment,
London, EC4Y 0DZ

GOOD LUCK!

Competition Entry Page

Please enter your details below:

1. Name of Frankie Book: ....
         Animal: ....

2. Name of Frankie Book: ....
         Animal: ....

3. Name of Frankie Book: ....
         Animal: ....

My name is: ....
My date of birth is: ....
Email address: ....
Address 1: ....
Address 2: ....
Address 3: ....
County: ....
Post Code: ....

Parent/Guardian signature: ....

FRANKIE'S MAGIC FOOTBALL WEBSITE

Have you had a chance to check out **frankiesmagicfootball.co.uk** yet?

Get involved in **competitions**, find out **news** and **updates** about the series, play **games** and watch **videos** featuring the author, **Frank Lampard!**

Visit the site to join **Frankie's FC** today!